177505

Two by Two

JOHN WINCH

HOLIDAY HOUSE / New York

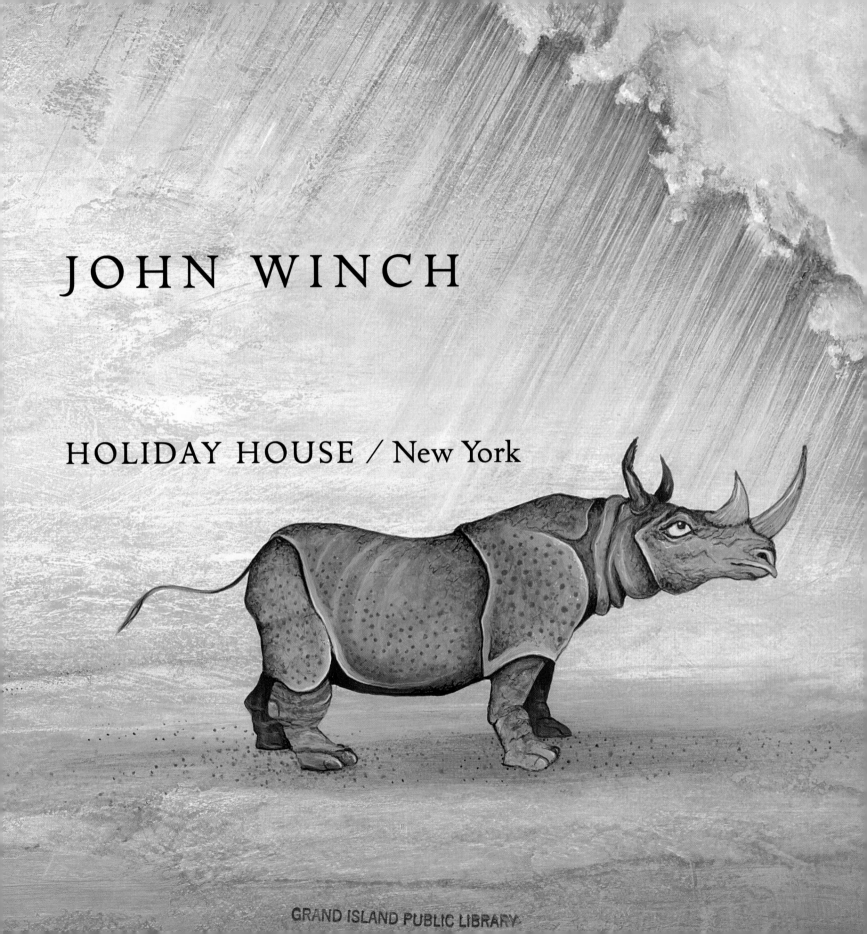

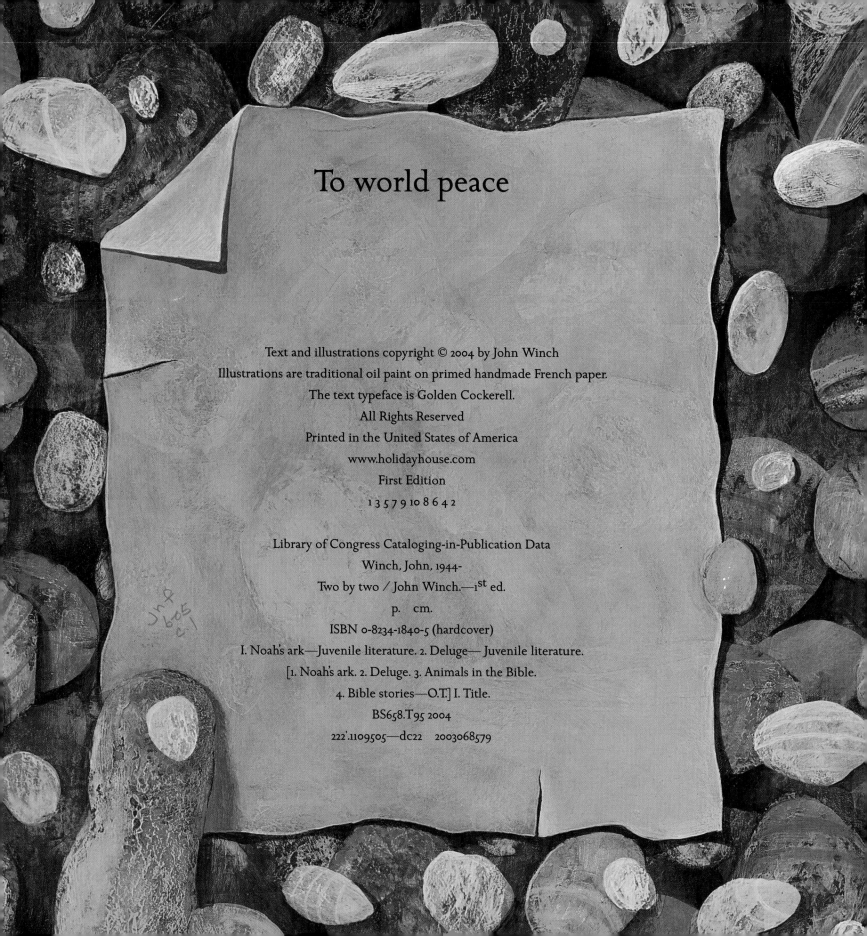

To world peace

Library of Congress Cataloging-in-Publication Data

Winch, John, 1944-

Two by two / John Winch.—1st ed.

p.   cm.

ISBN 0-8234-1840-5 (hardcover)

1. Noah's ark—Juvenile literature. 2. Deluge— Juvenile literature.

[1. Noah's ark. 2. Deluge. 3. Animals in the Bible.

4. Bible stories—O.T.] I. Title.

BS658.T95 2004

222'.1109505—dc22   2003068579

Long ago when the animals lived
happily together in peace,

they spent long days looking
for food, companions . . .

and a warm place
to sleep.

One day darkness fell on the earth. Wild winds blew. Lightning flashed across the sky, and claps of thunder echoed over the mountains, valleys, and plains. It began to rain.

It rained and rained until the rivers overflowed.

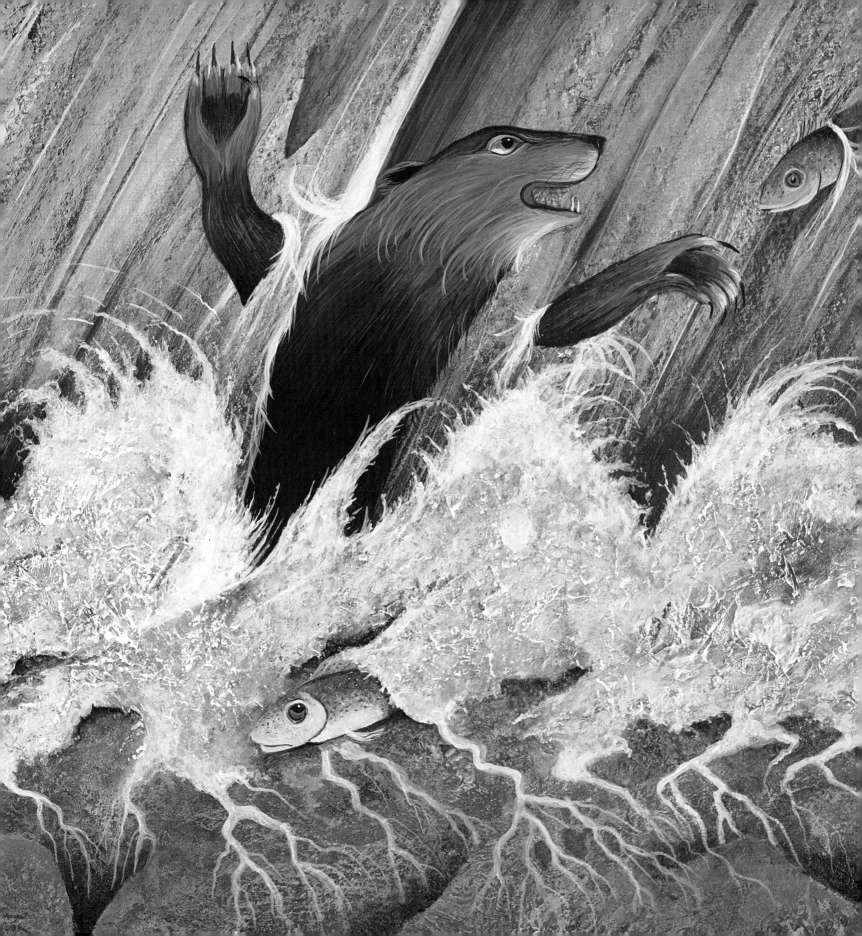

Water flooded the plains
and deserts.

Jungles vanished.

The North Pole and
South Pole disappeared.

Finally the tallest mountain peaks were covered

with water.

Small villages and
great cities were destroyed.

Some proud animals did not want help until the very last minute.

A few were almost lost.

Finally, there was only one dry, warm place left.

At last, when there was
no rain left to fall,
the sun shone.

Light and warmth
and freedom
returned
to the earth.

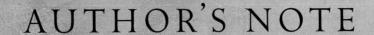

AUTHOR'S NOTE

More than three hundred cultures throughout the world contain a story of a great flood in their distant past. Some of these stories have been handed down by word of mouth from generation to generation, while others have been inscribed on clay tablets in picture writing or carved in lost languages on hard stone slabs and ancient walls. Fragile parchments painted thousands of years ago depict turbulent waters covering the earth and destroying cities and civilizations. Holy Scripture tells of a man named Noah and his family who survive a great deluge in a grand ark with two of every animal then inhabiting the earth. All the stories vary considerably in the characters involved, the period, the location, and the extent and consequence of the flood. However, they all have in common a theme of the earth being cleansed of man's evil and the rebirth of goodness.

Scientists and historians for centuries have excavated cities and the countryside and found evidence of a great flood, while others claim the deluge stories are merely fiction or folklore that have spread from one culture to the next. Modern people are constantly searching for remains of the great ark of these stories to either confirm or disprove the stories. They climb to the top of the tallest mountains in their quest to find the ark, scan the earth from satellites in space, and debate endlessly on the evidence discovered. No doubt the speculation will continue for generations to come, and more evidence of great floods will be unearthed and new stories will unfold. *Two by Two* could well be one of those stories yet to be found.

J. W. 2003.